The Red Bird

The Red Bird

BY ASTRID LINDGREN

TRANSLATED BY PATRICIA CRAMPTON

ILLUSTRATED BY MARIT TÖRNQVIST

ARTHUR A. LEVINE BOOKS ✦ AN IMPRINT OF SCHOLASTIC INC.

LONG AGO, in the days of poverty, there were two little children who were left alone in the world. But children cannot be alone in the world, they have to live with someone, and that was how Matthew and Anna from Sunnymead came to live with the farmer at Myra. He did not take them in because they had the clearest, gentlest eyes and the most faithful little hands, or because they were dazed with grief for their dead mother, no, he took the children to make themselves useful. Children's hands can work very well as long as they are not allowed to whittle bark-boats and carve whistles and build dens in the hillsides; children's hands can milk the Myra cows and clean out the oxen; children's hands can do anything as long as they are kept away from bark-boats and dens and all the things they really enjoy doing.

"I shall never have any more fun in my life," said Anna, crying as she sat on the milking stool.

"No, here in Myra all the days are as gray as the mice in the barn," said Matthew.

In the days of poverty, there was very little food in the farmsteads, and in any case the Myra farmer did not believe that children's stomachs needed anything but potatoes dipped in herring brine.

"My life won't be long," said Anna. "With potatoes and herring brine, I shan't live till winter."

"But you must live till winter," said Matthew. "In the winter you can go to school and the days will no longer be as gray as the mice in the barn."

When spring came to Myra, Matthew and Anna did not build
waterwheels in the streams or sail bark-boats in the ditches. They
milked the Myra cows and cleaned out the oxen, they ate potatoes
dipped in herring brine and cried a great deal when no one was
watching.

"If only I can live till winter and go to school," said Anna.

When summer came to Myra, Matthew and Anna did not pick fruit in the hedges or build dens in the hillsides; they milked the Myra cows and cleaned out the oxen, they ate potatoes dipped in herring brine and cried a great deal when no one was watching.

"If only I can live till winter and go to school," said Anna.

When autumn came to Myra, Matthew and Anna did not
play hide-and-seek among the sheds at dusk, and they did not sit
under the kitchen table whispering stories to one another in the
evening; no, they milked the Myra cows and cleaned out the
oxen, they ate potatoes dipped in herring brine and cried a great
deal when no one was watching.

"If only I can live till winter and go to school," said Anna.

In the days of poverty, children went to school for only a few weeks in wintertime. A traveling schoolteacher would appear from somewhere and settle himself in a little house in the village, and the children would come from all around to learn to read and count.

The Myra farmer, for his part, thought school was the silliest idea, and if only he could, he would have kept the children at home on the farm, but not even the Myra farmer could do that. You can keep children away from bark-boats and dens and wild strawberries, but you cannot keep them away from school, or the village priest will come and tell you, "Matthew and Anna must go to school!"

And winter came to Myra, the snow fell, and the drifts almost covered the windows of the barn. In the gloom of the barn Matthew and Anna danced together for sheer joy, and Anna said, "To think that I did live till winter and I shall be starting school tomorrow!"

And Matthew said, "Hey, all you barn mice, the gray days at Myra are over now."

When they came into the kitchen that evening, the farmer said, "School, that's as may be! But God help you if you're not home by milking time."

In the morning, Matthew and Anna took each other by the hand and walked off to school. It was a long way to walk, and in those days there was no one who cared if the way to school was short or long. The wind was icy, and Matthew and Anna were so cold that their toenails cracked and the tips of their noses turned quite red.

"Your nose is all red, Matthew," said Anna, "and that's lucky, otherwise you would be as gray as the mice in the barn."

They certainly were gray as mice, both Matthew and Anna, with the gray of poverty in their faces, the gray of poverty in their clothes: gray the shawl over Anna's shoulders, and gray the rough, homespun jersey passed on to Matthew by the Myra farmer. But now at least they were on their way to school and there would be no grayness there, thought Anna. At school there was sure to be the rosiest happiness from morning till night. So it didn't matter if they walked the timber track through the forest like two little gray mice and froze so pitifully in the harsh winter weather.

But going to school was not quite as much fun as they had thought. Of course it was nice to sit in a ring around the open stove with other children from the village and spell out the letters, but on the second day the schoolmaster had already hit Matthew across the fingers with his cane because he was not sitting still, and when it was time to eat their lunch packet, both Matthew and Anna were ashamed. Where they had only a few cold potatoes, the other children had bacon or cheese sandwiches, and Joel, the grocer's boy, had pancakes, a whole bundle of pancakes. Matthew and Anna stared at Joel's pancakes until their eyes grew shiny, and Joel said, "Little paupers, never seen food before?" Then Matthew and Anna sighed and were ashamed and turned away without answering.

No, the grayness did not vanish as they had believed, but they walked faithfully to school every day, although the snow lay in drifts along the timber track and their frostbitten toes were painful, and although they were pauper children with no sandwiches or pancakes.

Every day the Myra farmer said, "God help you if you're not home by milking time."

And Matthew and Anna did not dare get back too late for milking; they ran through the wood like two little gray mice on the way to their mousehole, they were so frightened of being too late.

But one day Anna stopped on the path and gripped Matthew's arm hard.

"Matthew," she said, "school didn't help. There is no fun in my life, and I don't want to live till spring."

She had just spoken when they saw the red bird. He was standing on the ground, so red against the white snow, so fiery, fiery red against the white. And his song rang out so clearly that the snow on the branches shattered into a thousand snow stars

that fell softly and silently to the ground.

Anna stretched out her hands toward the bird and wept.

"He's red," she said, "oh, he is red!"

Matthew cried too and said,

"He does not even know that there are gray mice in the world."

Then the bird spread his red wings and flew. Anna held Matthew tightly by the arm and said:

"If the bird flies away from me, I will lie down here in the snow and die."

So Matthew took her hand and they ran after the bird. He flew like the reddest torch through the fir trees, and wherever he flew the snow stars fell to the ground quite softly and silently, so piercing was the bird's song as he flew.

Straight into the wood they went, farther and farther from the path they ran, hither and thither flew the bird. Anna and Matthew struggled behind through the drifts, twigs struck their faces, and they tripped over stones hidden under the snow, but their eyes were alight with eagerness as they followed the bird.

Then all at once he disappeared.

"Unless I find the bird again, I will lie down here in the snow and die," said Anna.

Matthew comforted her. He patted her cheek and said,

"I hear the bird singing on the other side of the mountain."

"How do we get to the other side of the mountain?" asked Anna.

"Through that dark crevice there," said Matthew, and taking her hand, he drew her with him through the crevice. On the white snow in the depths of the crevice lay a red, shining feather, so they knew they were on the right path.

The crevice grew narrower, until at last it was so narrow that only a child's small body could squeeze through.

"The way is narrow," said Matthew, "but we are thinner still."

"Yes, the Myra farmer has seen to it that my poor little body can slip through anywhere," said Anna.

And then they were on the other side of the mountain.

"Now we are on the other side of the mountain," said Anna, "but where is my red bird?"

Matthew stood still in the wintry wood and listened.

"Behind the wall," he said, "he's singing behind the wall there."

There in front of them was a high wall and in the wall was a door. The door stood ajar, as if someone had just gone through and forgotten to close it behind him. The snow lay on the ground in drifts and the winter's day was frosty and cold, but over the wall a cherry tree stretched out its flowering white branches.

"We had cherry trees at home in Sunnymead as well," said
Anna, "but even there they didn't flower in winter."

Matthew took Anna by the hand and they walked through
the door.

And there they saw the red bird, he was the first thing they saw. He was sitting in a birch tree, and the birch tree had little green curly leaves, and it was spring. All the loveliness of spring burst over them in one exultant instant: A thousand little birds sang, rejoicing in the trees; all the spring rivulets gurgled, all the spring flowers sparkled, and children were playing in a meadow as green as the fields of paradise. Yes, many children were playing there, they had carved themselves bark-boats and were sailing them in the brooks and ditches, and they had cut whistles on which they played, so that they sounded like starlings in the spring. And they wore red and blue and white clothes that sparkled like spring flowers in the green grass.

"They don't even know that there are gray mice in the world," said Anna sadly. But at the same moment she saw that Matthew too was wearing red clothes, she herself was wearing red clothes, they were no longer as gray as the mice in the barn.

"This is the most wonderful thing that has happened to me in my whole life," said Anna. "What is this place I have come to?"

"You have come to Sunnymead," said the children playing in the brook nearby.

"Sunnymead, that's where we used to live, before our mouse-life in Myra began," said Matthew. "But it didn't look like this."

The children laughed.

"Then it must be a different Sunnymead," they said.

And they let Matthew and Anna play with them. Matthew
whittled a bark-boat and Anna made a sail of the red feather the
bird had dropped, and they launched their boat in the stream
and it sailed away with its red feather, the merriest of all the
bark-boats.

They built a waterwheel too, which whirred around in the
sunshine, and they paddled barefoot in the stream and felt
smooth sand under their feet.

"Smooth sand and soft grass, that's what my little feet like,"
said Anna.

Then they heard a voice calling, "Come, all my children!"

Matthew and Anna looked up from their waterwheel.

"Who is that calling?" said Anna.

"Our mother," said the children. "She wants us to come now."

"She won't want Anna and me to come," said Matthew.

"Oh yes, she will," said the children. "She wants all the children to come."

"But she is not our mother," said Anna.

"Oh yes, she is," said the children. "She is all the children's mother."

Then Matthew and Anna followed the other children across the meadow to a little cottage, and there was Mother. You could see that it was Mother, she had a mother's eyes and a mother's hands, and her eyes and hands were enough for all the children who crowded around her. She had cooked pancakes for them and she had baked bread, she had churned butter and she had made cheese, the children could eat as much as they liked of everything and they sat in the grass to eat.

"This is the best food I've eaten in my whole life," said Anna.

But Matthew suddenly turned pale and said,

"God help us if we're not home by milking time!"

Now they must hurry, now they remembered
they had been away much too long. They said
thank you for the food they had eaten and Mother
stroked their cheeks and said, "Come again soon!"

"Come again soon," said all the children,
following Matthew and Anna to the door in the
wall. It was still standing ajar, and they could see
the snowdrifts outside.

"Why isn't the door shut?" said Anna.
"The snow could blow in."

"Once the door shuts it can never be opened
again," said the children.

"Never again?" said Matthew.

"No, never, never again," said the children.

The red bird was still sitting in the birch tree
with its curly little green leaves that smelled as
good as birch leaves do in spring. But outside the
door the snow lay deep and the wood was frosty
and cold in the winter dusk. Matthew took Anna's
hand and they ran through the door. At once the
cold was upon them, and the hunger too; it was
as if they had never eaten pancakes and as if they
had never been given any bread.

The red bird flew ahead of them and showed
them the way, but in the chill winter dusk he no
longer glowed as red. Nor were their clothes red
anymore: The shawl that Anna pulled around
her shoulders was gray, and gray too the old
homespun jersey passed on to Matthew by
the Myra farmer.

So they came home at last and hurried to the barn to milk the Myra cows and clean out the oxen. When they went into the kitchen that evening, the farmer said:

"It's lucky that school stuff doesn't last forever."

But Matthew and Anna sat in a corner of the dark kitchen and talked for a long time about Sunnymead.

And they went on with their gray mouse-life in the Myra farmer's barn, but every day they went to school, and every day the red bird was sitting in the snow on the timber track and took them with him to Sunnymead. There they sailed their bark-boats, there they carved whistles for themselves and made their dens in the hillsides, and every day Mother gave them as much as they wanted to eat.

"If there were no Sunnymead, I would not give much for my poor life," said Anna.

But what the farmer said when they came into the kitchen
that evening was,

"Lucky that school stuff doesn't last forever. Afterward it'll be
staying home in the barn all day."

Matthew and Anna looked at each other and turned pale.

But the last day came, the last day of school and the last day of Sunnymead.

"God help you if you're not home by milking time," said the farmer, on the last day just like all the other days.

They sat by the stove at school and spelled out their letters for the last time. For the last time they ate their cold potatoes and smiled a little when Joel said, "Little paupers, never seen food before?" They smiled, because they were thinking of Sunnymead, where they would soon be fed.

And for the last time they came running along the timber path like two little gray mice. It was the coldest day of winter; white clouds of smoke rose from their mouths as they breathed and split nails hurt their fingers and toes. Anna wrapped the shawl as tight as she could about her shoulders and said, "I'm freezing and I'm hungry, I've never known anything worse in my young life."

It was so bitterly cold and they were longing so much for the red bird to lead them to Sunnymead. And then he was there, fiery red against the white snow. Anna laughed for joy when she saw him.

"So after all I can go one last time to my Sunnymead," she said.

The short winter's day was coming to an end, dusk was already falling, soon it would be night. But the bird flew like the reddest torch through the fir trees and sang as he flew so that a thousand snow crystals fell to the ground in the frosty, silent wood. The bird alone could be heard; so icy cold was it that the wood was silent, the pine trees' sighing song quelled by the cold.

Here and there flew the bird, Matthew and Anna struggling behind through the drifts, the way to Sunnymead was so long.

"My life will surely end here," said Anna. "The cold will take me before I can reach my Sunnymead."

But the bird flew ahead of them until at last they reached the door they knew so well. The snow lay deep outside, but the cherry tree stretched its flowering branches over the wall and the door stood ajar.

"Never have I longed so hard in my whole life," said Anna.

"But you are here now," said Matthew. "There is no more need for longing."

"No, I need not long anymore," said Anna.

And Matthew took her hand and led her through the door,
into the everlasting spring of Sunnymead, where the tender birch
leaves smelled so sweet, where a thousand small birds sang
joyfully in the trees, where the children sailed their bark-boats
in the spring brooks and ditches, and where Mother stood in the
meadow calling, "Come, all my children!"

Behind them lay the cold, frosty wood, and the winter night
was waiting. Anna looked out through the door into the darkness
and shuddered.

"Why is the door not closed?" she said.

"Oh, little Anna," said Matthew, "once the door is closed it can never be opened again, don't you remember that?"

"Oh yes, I remember that," said Anna. "Never, never again."

Then Matthew and Anna looked at one another. They looked
at one another for a long time, and then they smiled a little.
And then, very gently and quietly, they closed the door.